Always with you

Story by
Eric Walters

Art by
Carloe Liu

NIMBUS
PUBLISHING
NIMBUS.CA

For Peter, who left us too soon, and for Emily, the daughter
he left behind to carry on his essence. –E.W.

For Mandy, Lucas, and Derek. –C.L.

~

Nimbus Publishing Limited
3660 Strawberry Hill St, Halifax, NS B3K 5A9
(902) 455-4286 nimbus.ca

Printed and bound in China
NB1353
Editor: Penelope Jackson
Editor for the press: Whitney Moran
Design: Heather Bryan

Library and Archives Canada Cataloguing in Publication

Title: Always with you / story by Eric Walters ; art by Carloe Liu.
Names: Walters, Eric, 1957- author. | Liu, Carloe (Illustrator) illustrator
Identifiers: Canadiana 20189068124 | ISBN 9781771087384 (hardcover)
Classification: LCC PS8595.A598 A79 2019 | DDC jC813/.54—dc23

Nimbus Publishing acknowledges the financial support for its publishing activities from the Government of Canada, Canada Council for the Arts, and from the Province of Nova Scotia. We are pleased to work in partnership with the Province of Nova Scotia to develop and promote our creative industries for the benefit of all Nova Scotians.

A Note from the Author ⌒

Almost everybody has lost somebody they love. This story is about both love and loss. It is inspired by the loss of somebody who was very loved by my family.

In 2006 my brother-in-law Peter Mednis passed away leaving behind the two most important people in his life, his wife, Christine, and eleven-year-old daughter, Emily. Peter was a big, kind, larger-than-life, goofy guy. He didn't seem to have an "inside voice" and the ground almost shook as he walked by. His passing left behind a hole as big as he was. Not just for his wife and daughter, but for my wife, our children, myself, Peter's parents, and his wide range of friends. Peter was, by nature, somebody who could only see the best in people. That's probably why so many loved him.

Years later, when Emily was graduating from high school, two of Peter's long-time friends, Marc Stevens and Kenny Fukushima, wanted to give Emily a present "from Peter." It was a silver bracelet. That bracelet was the beginning of this story.

Always With You is my gift to Emily. Emily is more than just Peter's daughter; she is his legacy. And although he is gone, Emily knows he is always with her. I hope that as you read this book, you remember someone you love and all the ways they are still with you.

Emily woke. On her night table, a letter was propped against her grandfather's picture. Her name was printed in pencil crayon the way only Grandpa did it, with each letter a different colour.

He was always so kind and funny and silly…and now he was gone.

Carefully, she picked up the envelope and opened it.

Winter turned to spring, and the flowers in Grandpa's garden plot began to bloom. He used to nurture and care for those flowers the way he did for everyone around him. He was never far from Emily's thoughts, which made her happy and sad.

Spring turned to summer, and one day an envelope
came in the mail....

It held two season passes for the
amusement park where she and
Grandpa had gone so often!

Included was a small note.

When she rode the first roller coaster that year, she remembered that Grandpa always screamed louder than anybody. Heading down the first drop, she screamed so loud she *knew* he could hear her.

Time passed and that young girl started high school. Emily sat in the cafeteria on her first day, noise all around, surrounded by hundreds and hundreds of kids she didn't know.

She opened her lunch, and there beside the sandwich was a small parcel with her name on it. Her mother must have slipped it in.

Inside the parcel were a letter and a gold pen.

Emily held the pen and smiled...

...and a girl with green hair two tables over
smiled back at her.

Time passed and that high-schooler was about to graduate university. Emily tripped slightly as she climbed the steps, recovered, and then walked across the stage to accept her degree.

When she left the stage, her mother and father hugged her.

"You know how proud we are of you...*all* of us," her mother said. Her father handed her a small parcel.

Emily had seen her parents in the audience and felt her grandpa in her heart. She knew he had been there watching over her, making sure she didn't fall on the stairs. She opened the parcel. It was a silver bracelet. She removed it from the box and her mother helped her put it on her wrist.

"Your grandfather asked us to give it to you today. He had it inscribed."

Emily read the inscription. She knew in her heart what she saw with her eyes.

Time passed and that university graduate was about to be married. Emily took a deep breath and listened to the organ music. It was almost time for her mother and father to walk her down the aisle. Through the doors were all the people in the world who were important to her—including her husband-to-be.

Emily's father handed her a small parcel that she suspected would be coming.

Inside was her grandfather's pocket watch.

Time passed and that bride became a mother.

"Here," Emily's mother said. "For you and your newborn son."

Emily recognized the printing on the parcel. The letters had faded with time, but the love hadn't. She opened it to reveal a card and a silver rattle.

Emily picked up the rattle and gently shook it. Her brand new son seemed to turn ever so slightly toward the sound. She felt tears of joy form in her eyes.

"I know we haven't decided on a name," Emily said to her husband, "but I was just wondering if...."

He smiled. "If our son could be named after your grandfather?"

He was like her grandpa in so many ways. He always knew what she was thinking.

She nodded.

"I can't think of a better name," he said.

Emily looked into her baby's eyes and felt her grandfather's endless love pouring through her into this new little person. Then she said the only thing on her mind.

"Remember, darling,
I'll always be with you."